HOW MONTY FOUND HIS MAGIC

First published 2017 by Walker Books Ltd, 87 Vauxhall Walk, London
SE11 5HJ • This edition published 2019 • 10 9 8 7 6 5 4 3 2 1 •
© 2017 Lerryn Korda • The right of Lerryn Korda to be identified as
author/illustrator of this work has been asserted by her in accordance
with the Copyright, Designs and Patents Act 1988 • This book has been
typeset in Futura Book • Printed in China • All rights reserved. No part
of this book may be reproduced, transmitted or stored in an information
retrieval system in any form or by any means, graphic, electronic or
mechanical, including photocopying, taping and recording, without prior
written permission from the publisher. • British Library Cataloguing in
Publication Data: a catalogue record for this book is available from the
British Library • ISBN 978-1-4063-7897-9 • www.walker.co.uk

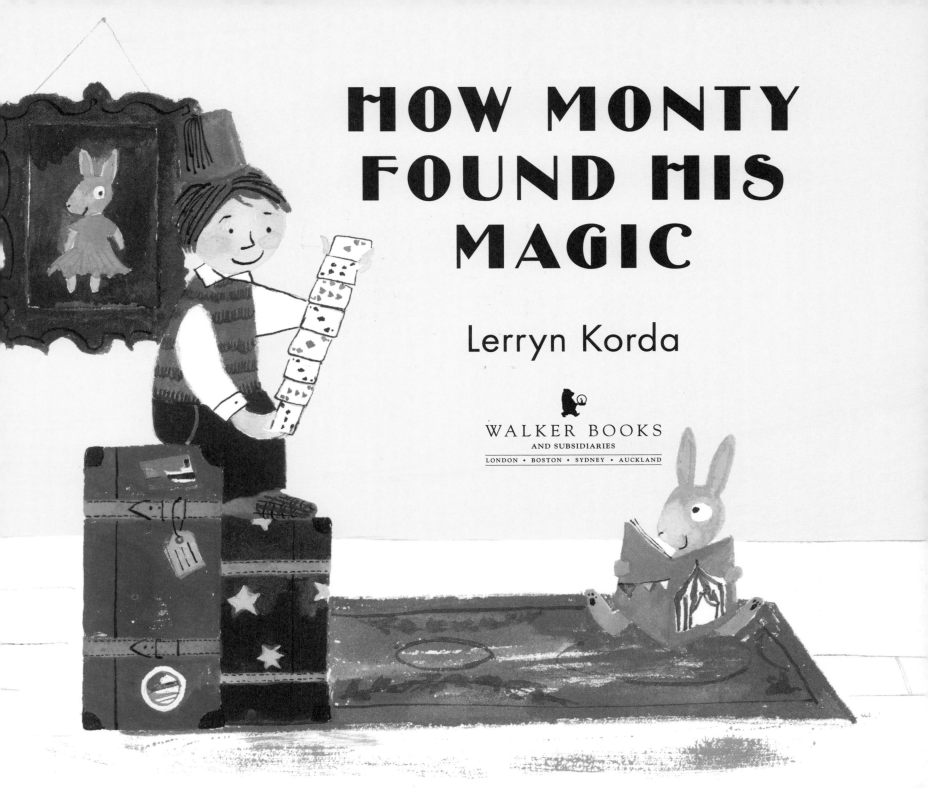

HOW MONTY FOUND HIS MAGIC

Lerryn Korda

WALKER BOOKS
AND SUBSIDIARIES

LONDON · BOSTON · SYDNEY · AUCKLAND

In quite a small house in a great big city lived three friends. A little boy called **Monty**, a rabbit called **Snuffles** ...

and a dog called **Zephyr**.

Monty, Snuffles and Zephyr
might look ordinary, but
together they were ...

The Magnificent Marvelloso Trio!

They dazzled with their Hair-Raising Hat Trick,

they razzled with their
Snake-Charming String Trick,
and they whirled and they twirled
and they shimmied and they swirled
before doing their Supernatural
Sawing-in-Half Trick ...

and they dreamed of
razzling and dazzling a
real audience one day.

ICE CREAM

The only problem was that whenever Monty tried to perform a magic trick in the outside world, he got so many butterflies in his tummy, he just couldn't do it.

Zephyr wished he knew how to help Monty feel marvellously magical all the time.

MR TWINKLES' TWINKLING
TALENT SHOW

Then, one day, Zephyr found just what he was looking for – a chance for Monty to show everyone how brilliant he really was.

But Monty was not so sure.

"Don't worry," said Zephyr. "We'll be **together**."

When they were home,

Zephyr and Snuffles got on the phone.

The very next day an important letter arrived in the post:

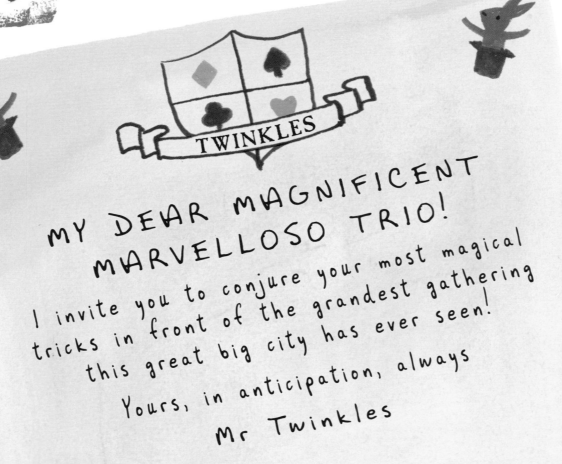

TWINKLES

MY DEAR MAGNIFICENT MARVELLOSO TRIO!

I invite you to conjure your most magical tricks in front of the grandest gathering this great big city has ever seen!

Yours, in anticipation, always

Mr Twinkles

On the morning of Mr Twinkles'
Talent Show, Monty had so many butterflies
fluttering in his tummy, he couldn't get out of bed.

"Don't worry," said Snuffles. "We're a bit nervous, too."

"But we'll be fine," said Zephyr. "Because we'll be **together**."

Zephyr and Snuffles made a special breakfast bursting with all their favourite magical combinations!

Monty tried on lots of silly costumes until he found one that was just right.

Then they got
to Mr Twinkles'
Talent Show just
about on time...

It was Monty and Snuffles

and Zephyr's turn to go on stage.

There were so many talented poodles

and pirouetting pandas, the butterflies in Monty's

tummy fluttered faster than ever.

Then Mr Twinkles called out, "Ladies and

gentlemen, please put your hands together for ..."

"The Magnificent Marvelloso Trio!"

All three friends went very, very quiet. The audience waited and they waited.

"I can't do it," whispered Zephyr.

"I don't think I can, either," said Snuffles.

Even though the butterflies in Monty's tummy were whizzing about and his heart was thumping fast, he knew just what to say...

"Yes, you can," said Monty. "Come on, let's do this **together**."

Monty and Snuffles and Zephyr conjured up all their courage and marched out onto the stage.

Together they performed their Hair-Raising Hat Trick, their Snake-Charming String Trick, and they whirled and they twirled and they shimmied and they swirled before doing their Supernatural Sawing-in-Half Trick!

Then the moment came for ...

ABRACADABRA ABRACA—

BOOOM!

Their very best trick of all!

The audience went wild with applause!

And, as if by magic, the butterflies in Monty's tummy vanished.

After all that, as I'm sure you can imagine, The Magnificent

Marvelloso Trio could do absolutely anything –

whether inside the comfort of their home ...

or outside in the big wide world ...

just as long as they were **together**.